DUTCH DOUBLE

Dear Becky—
May your heart
always see clearly!
Fran & Faye

FRAN GORDON & FAYE TISCHLER

INKWATER PRESS

PORTLAND • OREGON
INKWATERPRESS.COM

Copyright © 2007 by Fran Gordon & Faye Tischler

Cover & interior designed by Tricia Sgrignoli/Positive Images

Cover photograph of Lawrence the Indian by Herb Dieck
Button necklace provided by Fran Gordon & Faye Tischler

www.inkwaterpress.com

ISBN-10 1-59299-242-0
ISBN-13 978-1-59299-242-3

Publisher: Inkwater Press

Printed in the U.S.A.

SPECIAL THANKS

This book has been a labor of love and could not have been written without the help of many people. First and foremost are our husbands, Jim and Gene, for their unwavering support and faith in this project. All of our family members have continuously encouraged us and have helped to develop ideas as the story unfolded. Thank you all for everything you have done. Our colleagues at Paige School, especially Becky Hudak and Susan Cromer, listened patiently and helped us revise and edit, more than once! Thanks for the generous gift of your time and expertise. Additional editing support came from Esther Willison and Jeanne Finley. Their guidance in the fine art of commas, capitals, and content was invaluable! The cover photograph of Lawrence the Indian was taken by Herb Dieck who graciously gave us permission to use it. A special thanks goes to the many students who inspired this book and who listened and loved it.

CONTENTS

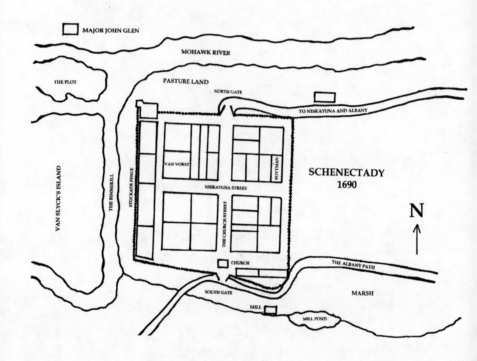

MAJOR JOHN GLEN

MOHAWK RIVER

THE PLOT

PASTURE LAND

NORTH GATE

TO NISKAYUNA AND ALBANY

VAN SLYCK'S ISLAND

THE BINNEKILL

STOCKADE FENCE

VAN VORST

POTTMAN

NISKAYUNA STREET

SCHENECTADY
1690

N

THE CHURCH STREET

CHURCH

THE ALBANY PATH

SOUTH GATE

MARSH

MILL

MILL POND

PROLOGUE

Schenectady is a small city in upstate New York. The community was established in the 1600's by fifteen Dutch families, who came from nearby Albany. These settlers came to farm the lands along the Mohawk River and to trade with the Mohawk Indians for valuable beaver furs.

The Dutch found the Mohawks, the eastern most Iroquois tribe, friendly and helpful. But even so, life for these early settlers was difficult. Enemy attacks and wild animals were constant dangers. By 1690, a stockade fence had been built around the perimeter of the settlement, and a few English soldiers were garrisoned inside the stockade to help protect the people living there.

That year French soldiers, with the help of enemy Iroquois, attacked the small settlement on a blizzardy February night. In spite of warnings, the Dutch were unprepared for the attack. Sixty settlers died in the massacre that followed, and much of the settlement burned to the ground.

None of the original seventeenth century homes in Schenectady survive, but the Stockade neighborhood, containing many houses built after 1690, exists at the same site today.

THE BIRTHDAY GIFT

Katie felt her heart sink. She had been dropping hints for weeks, but she knew the box in her father's hand was too small to be the new camera she wanted for her birthday. Looking at her father, Katie could see that he was excited about this gift he had chosen for her thirteenth birthday, but she was disappointed, and it was hard to pretend it didn't matter.

She glanced around the table where the Van Epps family was gathered to celebrate her birthday. *I'll bet Anna had something to do with this*, Katie thought. *It was so much better without her. Dad would have known what I wanted.*

"Come on, Katie, open your present!" Anna smiled brightly at Katie from her place right next to Katie's father at the dinner table. Katie pretended not to hear.

"Yeah, Dorp," said her brother Gerritt. "Hurry up so we can all eat. I'm starving." Seventeen-year old Gerritt had called her "Dorp" for as long as she could remember. When she was younger, she didn't know what it meant. She thought Gerritt was calling her the worst name in the world. Now Katie knew that "Dorp" was really a Dutch word for town, and "Old Dorp" was a nickname for Schenectady. But when she was little, the more upset she got,

1

the more he enjoyed torturing her with it. The nickname stuck.

"Dorp?" repeated Nikki Fadden, Katie's good friend, with a puzzled look. She had joined them for the birthday celebration.

"It's a long story," Katie muttered, and her eyes traveled back to the little box in her father's hand. He carefully placed the gift in front of her.

"I hope you like this. It was in your mother's family for years. We planned to give it to you together when you turned thirteen, but..." His voice trailed off.

Katie swallowed hard. Her mother, Martha, had been gone for three years, but it was still difficult for them to talk about it. The whole family seemed to avoid the subject. Anna, Katie's new stepmother, gently put her hand on her husband's arm. Katie quickly looked away. She had to fight back the anger she always felt whenever she saw the two of them together.

With all hopes for the camera gone, Katie unwrapped the package politely, deciding she wasn't going to like whatever it was. Taking the lid off the box, she reached under the fluffy white cotton and lifted out a shiny round button that hung at the end of a delicate gold chain, making it into a necklace. The button, polished until it shone, looked very old. Holding it close, Katie could see that it was made of gold with a raised tulip design on a lacy background. Even though Katie didn't share her father's enthusiasm for "old stuff," she had to admit this necklace was kind of pretty. Watching the button twirl gently at the end of its chain, she had the strangest feeling that it was somehow familiar. Where had she seen it before?

"Hey, Dorp," Gerritt's voice interrupted her thoughts. "Let me see that. I don't know many people who get an old button for a birthday present." Trying hard not to laugh, Gerritt turned to his father. "Dad, what do you have in mind for my birthday? Old shoelaces or something? I can hardly wait!"

Everyone at the table laughed except Katie, who was still trying to remember where she had seen that button before. Mr. Van Epps looked over his glasses at Gerritt disapprovingly, then cleared his throat and tapped on his water glass with his knife. He said, "If I can have everyone's attention, please! For your information, this is not just any old button. As a matter of fact, this button goes back eleven generations in your mother's family."

Gerritt, who loved history, looked at his father with sudden interest. "Dad, do you mean to tell me that this button goes back to our...let's see," he said, counting slowly on his fingers, "great-great-great-great-great-great-great-great-great-great-great-grandmother?"

"That's too many greats to keep track of," complained Katie. "I'll just call her my TOO many great-grandmother."

Nikki leaned over to Katie and in a whisper said, "What's with all of this old stuff? In my family my mother didn't even keep my baby clothes. I'll bet the oldest thing you'd find in our house is yesterday's newspaper!" Katie giggled and gave her friend a quick kick under the table as her father continued his speech.

"This button, Katie, has been worn by different women in your mother's family since the early Dutch days of Old Schenectady. Your mother's maiden name was Martha Vroman as you know, but we traced her family back to the

Van Vorsts who were one of the first families to settle in Schenectady."

Katie found herself only half listening as her father once again started telling the familiar story about her Dutch ancestors who were such an important part of Schenectady's early history. She'd heard the same story many times before.

"You realize that not everyone back in the 1600's could even afford buttons," her father continued. "They were a sign of wealth at that time. Buttons were important enough for people to pass them on to their children when they died." Mr. Van Epps paused. "And that's how this button has come to you, Katie. It belonged to your mother, but...it's also a link to your past. Do you understand what I mean?" His eyes searched Katie's face for a sign that she understood how important this gift was.

Katie's mind was a jumble of thoughts. She was still disappointed about the camera, but she had to admit, in spite of herself, this was a very special gift. After all, it had been her mother's. Katie felt the lump growing in her throat again. Swallowing hard, she managed a weak smile.

"Thanks Dad, I really like it." As Anna reached towards Katie to help fasten the necklace, Katie leaned away and quickly added, "Would you help me put it on, Dad?" Katie knew that she had hurt Anna's feelings, but she decided not to think about it.

At that moment, Nikki reached over and touched the necklace that Katie now wore. "That looks pretty, Kate," she said.

"Hey, I just thought of something!" Nikki said excitedly. "Maybe our ancestors knew each other. You know I'm part Native American, right? My father's family is

Iroquois, from the Mohawk tribe, I think. They were around back then, weren't they, Mr. Van Epps?"

"Yes, they certainly were, Nikki. As a matter of fact, the Mohawk Valley was their home long before the Dutch got here. I'm not surprised that you and Katie are such good friends," he added laughingly. "The Dutch and the Mohawks always got along well."

"C'mon you guys," pleaded Gerritt. "Enough history, even for me! Can we eat now?"

The old grandfather clock in the hallway was chiming eight when Katie walked Nikki to the front door. "Great dinner, Kate," said Nikki. "Thanks for inviting me." She straightened up after tugging on her boots and yanked a colorful knit cap down over her long black hair. Turning to Katie with a serious look, Nikki said, "You should try to get along better with Anna. She's really not so bad, you know."

Katie's face turned hard. "You don't have to live with her...and your real mother's alive!" she snapped.

"I'm sorry," Nikki said quietly. "I guess it's really none of my business."

"Don't worry about it. I'm sorry too. It's just that everything's so changed for me. I wish it was still three years ago and things were like they used to be."

"It'll all work out, Kate," Nikki said softly as she pulled open the front door. "I'll call you tomorrow."

Katie closed the heavy wooden door and watched through the leaded glass of the window as Nikki disappeared past the statue of "Lawrence the Indian" and down North Ferry Street into the darkness. Resting her cheek against the cold glass, Katie's eyes were drawn back to the statue, looking lifelike in the dim glow of the streetlights.

So many things had changed in her life, but that statue of Lawrence had been there as long as she could remember, a reminder of the friendly Mohawk who had been helpful to the early Dutch settlers after the Massacre of 1690. Katie was always amazed to think that something like the Massacre had happened right here where she lived. She shivered as she thought about it. *Glad I didn't live here back then,* she thought. Sighing, she turned to go up the stairs to her room. Her hand gently touched the button hanging on its chain around her neck. Katie could picture her mother holding this same button. Having it in her own hand somehow seemed to bring her mother closer. Would things ever really be all right?

With the necklace still in her hand, Katie switched on the hall light at the bottom of the stairs. Nothing happened.

"Dad, the light's out in the hallway," Katie shouted.

"O.K. Katie, I'll fix it tomorrow," he called back over the clatter of dishes in the kitchen. "Just be careful going up the stairs."

Katie started up the gloomy staircase. Surprisingly, it wasn't as dark as she had expected. The familiar shapes of the old Van Epps and Van Vorst family portraits lined the walls, but she was startled to see that there was a hazy golden glow bathing one of the portraits. Stopping in front of it she tried to see more clearly, her eyes searching through the dim light.

What's going on? Katie thought.

She stepped closer. Suddenly she gasped as she realized that the glow was coming from a button in the portrait, a button that looked like the same golden button she was wearing on the chain around her neck! This woman must be the "too many" great grandmother her father and Gerritt had talked about at dinner! In the old oil painting, the button was worn not as a necklace, but was used to fasten the neck of a fancy cloak. "That's where I've seen it before!" Katie whispered with amazement, her hand gripping the button tightly.

With a jolt, Katie realized the button in her hand had become hot. She quickly took her hand away, feeling the button drop against her chest. It lay on its chain outside of her sweatshirt, but she could still feel its strange heat.

"Katie? Are you OK?" She turned towards her father's voice, which came from the bottom of the stairs. Katie forced her eyes back to the portrait, but the mysterious glow had disappeared. She reached out and slowly ran her fingers over the bumpy surface of the painting.

"I'm fine…I think," Katie said in a shaky voice.

"It's pretty dark on these stairs. Why did you stop?" Mr. Van Epps asked in a concerned voice.

"I don't know," Katie said softly, "I really don't know."

THE BIG DAY

It seemed to be happening again. The dull glow of the mysterious light on the stairway grew brighter and brighter, filling the space around her. She could feel the button on the chain around her neck becoming warm and tingly. When it continued to grow hotter, Katie clawed at it frantically. As the heat became unbearable against her skin, she tried to call for help, struggling to find her voice.

"Dad!" she called through the intense light. "Dad! The button… it's hot!"

Suddenly, she was wide-awake, sitting up in her own bed with bright sunlight streaming into the room.

It was just a bad dream, she thought. With trembling hands she brushed the damp hair back from her face. Just to be sure, she fingered the button around her neck and was relieved to find that it was cool. Everything was O.K… wasn't it?

Hurrying to her bedroom window, Katie was reassured by the familiar sights and sounds of the Stockade streets. Her eyes rested on the snow-covered statue of Lawrence.

"Hey, Lawrence," she said cheerfully, as she had each morning for as long as she could remember. "I wonder what you were really like." Then, glancing at the clock and realizing that it was later than she thought, she hurried to shower and dress.

A short time later she bounced down the stairs ready to face the new day. She stopped when she saw her father at the bottom of the stairway holding a stepladder. "I just changed that bulb so you won't have to worry about it anymore," he said.

"Thanks, Dad," Katie said with relief. "It sure was spooky around here last night." She glanced at the portrait.

Mr. Van Epps looked at his daughter curiously then said, "Remember the photo shoot this afternoon, Katie."

"Oh no!" she groaned. "I forgot. It's today!" She quickly drew her eyes away from the portrait and shook her head. Her good mood vanished. She hated the colonial Dutch costume she had to wear for the celebration of Schenectady's tercentennial.

"Why should I care what it was like to live around here three hundred years ago?" she grumbled under her breath.

Anna had spent many hours making Katie's costume. Knowing that the Dutch did not like wearing dull colors, she made sure to use a dark blue wool with a lighter stripe running through it for the full skirt that was hemmed a few inches below Katie's knee. Anna also had made a matching bodice. With the costume, Katie wore bright blue knitted stockings with a red design, an apron, a lace cap and a heavy woolen cloak. Since pockets hadn't been invented in the 1600's, a pouch tied around her waist was used to hold small things. Dutch women called the pouch a "pocket". There was even a pair of klompen, or wooden shoes, for her feet. Hoping to make the costume a little more special for the reluctant Katie, Anna had sewn a shiny new coin, minted in 1990, into the hem of the skirt.

"Just for fun," Anna had laughed. "Maybe it'll even bring you good luck."

The costume was very similar to the clothes worn by Katie's "too many" great grandmother in the portrait in the hallway. Standing in front of it now, Katie once again began to feel uneasy as she realized the button was growing warmer. "Stop being silly," she said to herself firmly. "It's just your imagination!"

But she forgot all about the button once she was unwillingly caught up in the excitement around the tercentennial celebration. Her father had been put in charge of planning the city's special events to mark the three-hundredth anniversary of the Schenectady Massacre in 1690. On that date, the tiny settlement of Schenectady was left in ashes. Sixty people were killed, and almost thirty were taken captive by the enemy. Mr. Van Epps expected his whole family to be enthusiastically involved in remembering this important event.

It was an unusually mild day for February when Katie reluctantly walked with Anna down Front Street, her long skirt and cloak tangling themselves around her legs as she clumped along in the wooden shoes.

"Gerritt's the one who likes this stuff, not me. I feel so stupid!" Katie growled as she tugged at the lace cap on her head and angrily chewed a wad of gum. The cap threatened to fly away with every breeze, and she gave it a furious tug on both sides to make it stay.

"Hi, Mrs. Van Epps. Hey, Kate, you look great!" called a familiar voice.

Katie turned to find Nikki smiling cheerfully as she handed out maps to the growing crowd. Nikki thrust a map into Katie's hand. It showed the Dutch stockade area as it was in 1690.

"You won't believe who just took one of my maps," Nikki said excitedly. "It was the GOVERNOR!"

Without waiting for a reply from Katie, Nikki turned away and disappeared into the crowd. With a frown, Katie crumpled the map and jammed it into the "pocket" that was tied around her waist. She was still fuming at having been the student chosen to dress in Dutch costume for the publicity pictures. She had not been able to make her teacher understand how embarrassing it would be.

"But you are the obvious choice!" Mrs. Scampini had gushed with enthusiasm. "Just think about your Dutch heritage. You live in the historic Stockade area of Schenectady, in one of the oldest homes, and your father is such an expert on colonial Dutch history...."

Anna's voice interrupted Katie's thoughts. "You look great! So... authentic!" Anna said with a warm smile.

Katie ignored her. They were on their way to meet Katie's father at the site where the publicity photos were being taken. Giles Van Epps, as the foremost authority on colonial Dutch culture in Schenectady, was already there answering questions from newspaper and T.V. reporters.

"What is the big deal--this is so stupid!" Katie said as she and Anna walked along Front Street. She did not return Anna's smile. She would NEVER return Anna's smiles, she promised herself. This woman had no place in their lives, she wasn't family, she wasn't Katie's real mother. "Just because you and my Dad love this stuff about a bunch of old dead people," Katie said haughtily, "doesn't mean I have to! Like I said, it's stup...."

Her voice trailed off as they turned the corner onto Church Street. Her nose sniffed at a faint but familiar smell. The site marker identifying the gateway to the original stockade was facing them. And there, prancing nervously in place, with a wild-eyed look, was a large, real-life brown horse. Astride the horse was a man dressed as Lawrence the Indian. Katie felt terror flash through her body.

THE HORSE

"A horse...," Katie whispered. Hurt and anger swelled uncontrollably inside her, just as it had three years ago. "You knew," Katie hissed. "Why didn't you tell me?" She turned to a startled Anna, her eyes still riveted on the horse.

"Oh, Katie, I didn't know the horse would be here! Honestly I didn't!" Anna reached out to touch Katie's trembling arm.

"I hate you," Katie said, angrily pushing Anna's arm away, still watching the prancing horse. Unwelcome memories flooded in, and for a moment she was lost in time, three years ago. Her mother had been an expert rider who enjoyed competing for blue ribbons at horse shows. She wanted to share her love for horses with her daughter, so since the age of four Katie and her mother had been riding at a local stable where they kept their two horses, Star and Spirit. There was nothing Katie loved more than sharing a Saturday with her mother at the barn. Together they would laugh as they groomed the horses. The high point of the day was riding out on the trails together. Spirit was an excellent jumper and Katie always felt proud as she watched her mother and the horse sail over the jumps in perfect form. Martha had won many ribbons at the nearby county fairs that way. It was at one of these competitions that Katie's life was changed forever.

Katie saw it all again: Spirit suddenly refused to jump. He pawed the air, a wild look in his eyes. Katie watched her mother's frantic effort to stay on the bucking horse. She heard it all again--the scream, the chilling thud of her mother's body on the hard ground... the awful silence of the stunned crowd. They never found out why Spirit refused to jump that day.

Katie relived those moments every time she saw a horse. She had learned to avoid the terrible, sickening feelings that overwhelmed her, by never going near one. She never rode anymore. Her father sold both horses because they were too painful a reminder of what had happened.

For over a year after the accident, Katie's father had been sad and very quiet. But when he met Anna things started to change. He seemed happier and began to laugh more often. Katie hated it. Had he forgotten her mother?

"Anna! Katie!" Her father was approaching them, a big smile on his face. "Goeden dag," he said greeting them in Dutch with the only words in that language Katie understood. As usual he was so caught up in the excitement of the day, he hadn't noticed how upset Katie looked.

"Why didn't you tell me a horse would be here?" Katie yelled angrily at him, her voice loud and slightly hysterical. Katie suddenly became aware of a hush in the crowd. She thought all eyes were on her.

Giles Van Epps gathered his trembling daughter into his arms and said, "I'm so sorry, Katie, I should have known that this would upset you. I wasn't thinking. Let's get you out of here. Why don't you and Anna go and wait for me at…"

Before Giles Van Epps could finish, a rumpled-looking man, wearing a bow tie and carrying an old fashioned flash camera, pushed his way toward them through the crowd, calling, "Make way for the press, *Daily Gazette* here." He leaned forward, coming uncomfortably close to Katie. "I need a shot of the two of you," he said nodding briskly at Katie and the man dressed as Lawrence the Indian, who sat astride the horse. "I want to get the little lady up there on the horse with the Injun."

"No! You don't understand..." protested her father.

But Katie was already being propelled forward. She tried to pull away with all of her strength, when suddenly Lawrence's strong arm reached down and dragged her up behind him. In her fear she grabbed onto the rough fabric of the homespun shirt Lawrence was wearing as part of his costume. Katie found her face pressed close to the glossy black braids of his wig. She closed her eyes for a moment, unable to look down. She heard Lawrence speak in a soft, soothing voice to calm the nervous animal beneath them. As the skittish horse shifted its footing, Lawrence must have felt her trembling, because he looked at her over his shoulder with dark, reassuring eyes.

"Katie!" She heard her father call to her. She leaned down toward his outstretched hands.

A STRANGE JOURNEY

A blinding flash came without warning from the direction of the camera. Suddenly everything around Katie was lost in a wash of white light, tiny black dots swam before her eyes and the horse lunged forward. Katie screamed as she instinctively tightened her hold on Lawrence to keep from falling.

Hunched close to Lawrence's back, Katie could feel the powerful muscles of the horse moving beneath her. They seemed to be flying through a white haze. Cold air rushed by, making her body feel numb. Tiny particles of ice stung her cheeks as she became aware of the faint smell of pine trees and wood smoke. One sensation stood out: the button necklace, pressed against her chest as she clung to Lawrence, was burning hot!

Looking around, Katie realized that nothing looked familiar. Deep snow covered the ground, forcing the horse into an uneven gait. Tall pines grew everywhere along the rutted track they seemed to be following. The pines' graceful branches were bent under the weight of newly fallen snow. There were no houses, no people.

"Wh-What's going on?" Katie stammered.

Lawrence didn't answer, but turned the horse down a trail that appeared on their left. Ahead of them, rising out of the white landscape, was a tall, wooden stockade fence made from upright pointed logs.

"I don't understand," Katie said. "Where are we? I don't like this! Where's my father?"

But if Lawrence heard her, he chose to remain silent. Adding to her confusion, Katie realized that Lawrence's glossy black braids, so obviously a wig before, were definitely real now. He looked so different. On top of his head was a round hat decorated with feathers and porcupine quills. He had a fur-lined robe wrapped around his body.

By now they had come up to the log stockade. Turning abruptly, the horse cantered along the wall and came to a stop at a gate. A short, heavy man stepped forward, blocking their path. His clothing was unlike anything Katie had ever seen before except in her father's history books. He was wearing dark baggy pants that ended, and were gathered, at his knees. Below that he wore thick grey stockings that looked hand-knit. He was bundled up against the cold, and carried an antique-looking musket.

"Goeden dag, Lawrence," the man said gruffly, "What is your business here today?"

Reining in the horse alongside the watchman, Lawrence nodded back towards Katie. "I bring Katje to Mevrouw Van Vorst. New servant girl."

A second watchman appeared and stepped forward. "Ah, good," he said glancing at Katie, "Mevrouw Van Vorst has been waiting these many months to get some help. It's a shame that the poor woman was left alone with the five children and a tavern to run after the fever took her husband."

"Van Vorst? Did you say Van Vorst?" gasped Katie, "That name was in my mother's family!"

The two watchmen laughed. "There are many Van Vorst families, but none here are servants like you," the first watchman replied. They stepped aside as Lawrence urged the horse forward, through the gate and inside the stockade fence.

Katie listened with alarm. *They weren't speaking English! It sounded something like the Dutch Dad speaks,* she thought, *but why could I understand them?*

She began to take in her new surroundings. On either side of the rutted, muddy road, rows of small houses lined the street, their gabled ends facing front. Most of the houses were a combination of wood and stone and looked very old-fashioned. Smoke curled lazily from the brick chimneys atop the steep thatched and tiled roofs. Katie had the feeling that she had just stepped into an antique painting. It all seemed unreal, but the warmth of the button against her chest kept reminding her that she wasn't dreaming.

The horse continued slowly down the snow-packed street. It was mostly deserted. A two-wheeled wooden cart, pulled by a horse and loaded with wooden kegs, creaked past them going the other way. Standing on the stoop of one of the nearby houses were two heavily bundled children, both wearing red woolen cloaks and warm fur caps. The children stared at them with curiosity as the horse turned right onto the only other street in view.

Lawrence brought the horse to a stop in front of a wooden clapboard house. Anxiously Katie asked, "Why are we stopping here?"

Without answering, Lawrence swung his leg over the neck of the horse and slid to the ground. Turning, he reached up for Katie.

She asked in a small, frightened voice, "Where are we?"

Still silent, Lawrence lifted Katie from the horse and set her down in front of the house's heavy wooden door. After tying the horse to a nearby post, Lawrence banged loudly on the door and waited. Katie gathered her long woolen cloak tightly around her and shivered. The sun was sinking lower in the February sky. Though her body was chilled, Katie noticed the button still felt warm.

KATJE, NOT KATIE

The top half of the Dutch-style door scraped open and Katie and Lawrence were both greeted by a smiling face.

"Goeden avond," said a pleasant looking woman. Katie guessed she was probably around the same age as Anna. Her light brown hair was pulled back and covered by a cloth cap similar to the one that Katie still wore as part of her costume.

"Goeden avond, Mevrouw Van Vorst," Lawrence replied. "I bring Katje, new servant girl."

The woman smiled broadly. "We have been waiting for you to come live with us, Katje. There is much work to be done here. Come in, both of you, warm yourselves by the fire," she said pleasantly.

The top half of the door swung shut with a loud thud. A few seconds later, after bolting the two halves together inside, the woman flung open the whole door and motioned for Katie and Lawrence to step in. But Katie couldn't move. The woman had said "come live with us."

"Wait," stammered Katie. "There must be some mistake. I can't stay here!" But hearing a child crying somewhere in the back of the house, the woman had already turned away. Wheeling around quickly, Katie grabbed Lawrence's arm.

"Take me home! You know I don't belong here! Why is this all happening?"

Gently removing her hand, Lawrence seemed concerned by her fear. "It is not time," he said.

"What do you mean, 'time'? When will it be time?" Katie cried.

"Remember this," Lawrence said, turning away.

"When the snow covers the moon,
Your heart will see clearly.
The gateway to the past is the door to the future."

"Wait, don't leave me here! Please!" begged Katie, tears now streaming down her flushed face. She watched in despair as Lawrence easily mounted the horse and disappeared down the snowy street.

Katie felt an arm around her shoulders. "Poor child. You must have had a long journey. Come inside now."

Numb, Katie allowed herself to be led towards the crackling fire by the kind woman. As her eyes adjusted to the dimly lit room she saw that two small children had gathered behind the woman's skirt. They peeked out at her with wide eyes.

"Warm yourself at the fire, Katje. You must be hungry. I will bring you something to eat." She began to ladle a soupy stew into a red stoneware bowl. Katie clutched the cloak tightly around her shoulders. She was startled by a loud wail that came suddenly from a wooden cradle on the floor near the fire.

"If you pick up the child it will quiet her," suggested Mevrouw Van Vorst.

Not knowing what else to do, Katie bent down and lifted the crying baby out of the cradle. The baby, bundled in many layers of scratchy woven cloth, was hard to hold. Katie was relieved when Mevrouw Van Vorst took the baby and handed her the steaming bowl. The warmth of the bowl helped thaw her frozen fingers, but it wasn't very long before the food and warmth made Katie sleepy. As she struggled to keep her eyes open she hoped that all of this was just a bad dream.

The next morning, as light crept through a small window, Katie rolled over with a groan. Bits of straw poked at her through the lumpy mattress on the wooden plank floor. The events of yesterday flooded back. It hadn't been a dream, but what had really happened? How did she get here, and more importantly, how would she get home? *Dad must be really worried about me. He doesn't know where I am,* she thought tearfully. *I don't even know where I am.*

She looked around at her surroundings. She seemed to be in some kind of attic, or garrett, as Mevrouw Van Vorst had called it last night. Katie had been too tired to care where she slept when she stumbled up the steep ladder. It had been dark and cold when she crawled gratefully under the heavy feather-filled comforter.

Katie sat up and the first thing she noticed was another similar mattress to her left. It looked like someone had slept there because of the rumpled bedding. In a far corner of the garrett were several wooden barrels of different sizes. Leaning against the barrels were some bulging cloth sacks. In another corner Katie could make out the shapes of two large trunks shoved against the wall. Wet clothes were draped over long poles that hung from the rafters above.

Voices drifted up from the room below. "It can do no harm to let the child sleep, Cornelius. She had an exhausting journey yesterday." Katie recognized the firm voice of Mevrouw Van Vorst. The next voice was unfamiliar, but sounded like a young man.

"She is here to work Mother. She is a servant and I am afraid she will become spoiled."

"She will be busy soon enough," was the calm reply.

But Cornelius continued. "Wake Katje. It is time for her to eat."

What will I do? thought Katie. Taking a deep breath she said to herself, *Don't you dare fall apart Katie Van Epps! Just play along with these people until you understand what this is all about.*

Footsteps sounded on the ladder, and a few seconds later a young boy, who looked about ten years old, appeared at the top. They stared at each other.

"Goeden morgan, I am Pieter," he said importantly, climbing over the top of the ladder. "Are you hungry?"

From under his longish blonde hair, he smiled shyly. Pieter wore a blue wool vest over a long sleeved, white linen shirt. Katie thought that part wasn't so strange, but the pants the boy wore came to just below his knee. Long grey stockings, like heavy socks, covered the rest of his legs and feet.

Pieter was eyeing Katie with equal curiosity.

"I'm Katie Van Epps," she said. "I don't really under-stand what's going on here, but yeah, I guess I am hungry." Standing up, she self-consciously tried to smooth her long, rumpled skirt. "I don't usually sleep in my clothes, but I guess I was really tired last night, and it was so cold up here. Is there some place I can take a shower?"

"A shower?" the boy repeated, with a puzzled look. He turned abruptly and disappeared down the ladder.

The idea of a shower was quickly forgotten as Katie braced herself for what waited below. Taking a deep breath, she started down.

WHERE AM I?

At the bottom of the ladder Katie followed the sounds of voices down a short, narrow hallway to a back room. The voices stopped suddenly as she appeared in the doorway. Reminding herself to stay calm, her eyes traveled around the room, taking in her surroundings. Three children sat on a bench near the fireplace. It was different from the fireplaces Katie was used to seeing because it didn't have a mantle over it. Along side the bench an older teenager stood next to Mevrouw Van Vorst, who held the baby in her arms. In the far corner stood a bed that looked as if it had been built into a large cupboard-like space in the wall. Fancy embroidered cloth, hanging like curtains, partially hid a feather mattress. There was very little other furniture in the room except for some chests, a table and a tall dresser. On the wooden dresser were some pretty blue and white plates along with some pitchers and other silvery looking plates made out of pewter. Two spinning wheels stood next to a weaving loom in another corner of the small crowded room, one large and one small.

Looking up at the ceiling rafters Katie was surprised to see food hanging there: whole hams, chunks of bacon, sausages, dried meat. There were also strings of dried peppers, bunches of herbs, and ears of dried corn.

"Come warm yourself at the fire, child, I'll get you some porridge," said Mevrouw Van Vorst. Shyly looking at the children, Katie walked hesitantly toward them. Mevrouw Van Vorst suddenly thrust the chubby baby she held into Katie's arms and said, "Here, watch Helena." With that she turned to one of the kettles hanging in the huge fireplace and started to ladle something that looked like oatmeal into a red stoneware bowl. Katie held the squirming baby in her arms and wondered what she was supposed to do next. The heavy baby, bundled in layers of woven cloth, began to cry loudly.

"Can you not keep her quiet?" asked the older boy in a deep voice. He looked to be about fifteen or so. "That will be one of your jobs you understand," he continued.

Katie looked at him. He was standing by a large, high-backed bench that was pulled up close to the fire. "My jobs?" she repeated.

Mevrouw Van Vorst called to the children who were sitting on the bench, "Cornelius, let her eat. Pieter! You take Jan on your lap, and Christina, you slide over so that Katje can sit with you on the settle."

Katie was relieved to sit down with the baby. She thankfully took her place on the settle next to Christina, a small blonde girl of about four, who looked up at Katie with wide blue eyes. Mevrouw Van Vorst placed the porridge on the floor at Katie's feet. Katie was able to turn the fussing baby so that she was facing her. She bounced Helena up and down on her lap, hoping to stop her wailing. The glittering gold button that still hung around Katie's neck caught the baby's attention. Helena stopped crying and reached for the button with her pudgy fingers.

"What is it that Helena holds in her hand?" asked Pieter.

"It's a button that my father gave me as a gift," answered Katie, fighting back tears as she thought about how far away she must be from her own home.

"Where would a servant's family get something as valuable as a button?" asked Cornelius rudely.

"Cornelius!" interrupted Mevrouw Van Vorst in a sharp voice. "There is no need to speak that way to our servant."

"Servant!" Katie said, before she could stop herself. "I don't know anything about being a servant!" Then, hoping to find out where she was, she said, in an unsteady voice, "What is the name of this place? I can't seem to remember."

"Our settlement is called Schoonechtendel," replied Mevrouw Van Vorst.

Katie's heart pounded when she realized that this was the Dutch name that her father always used when he talked about early Schenectady. *Schoonechtendel?* It wasn't only the cold room that made Katie shiver. "Wh-wh-at is the date?" Katie asked, with growing fear.

"Why, it is the 6th day of February, in the year 1690!" Mevrouw Van Vorst answered in surprise. "Your trip must have really tired you to make you forget!"

Katie gasped. Was it possible? Had she traveled back in time somehow? Thoughts raced through her mind. If it was February 6th, 1690, that was only two days before The Massacre. They had just studied it in school. Schenectady was burned and lots of people got killed. She had to get out of here!

Katie asked anxiously, "Is Lawrence coming back for me?"

"No, child," said Mevrouw Van Vorst gently. "You must remember the paper you marked was your agreement to work for us as a servant for the next ten years."

Paper? Ten years! I never signed any paper, thought Katie with alarm. *If it's really February 6^{th,} I don't have ten years!*

RUMORS IN THE TAVERN

Katie had to quickly make herself believe that she was really living in the year 1690. Knowing she only had two days before the massacre would happen, her plan was to find Lawrence while she pretended to be the servant girl, Katje.

But pretending to be a servant was not an easy job. Katie found she had no time to look for Lawrence, because even her first day was filled with endless chores. Everybody in the family was expected to work around the house. Katie soon realized that part of the house was used as a tavern, a place where travelers and men from Schoonectendel gathered for food, drink and the latest news. Mevrouw Van Vorst and Cornelius spent most of their time tending to the tavern. The fires had to be kept burning, and there was always food to be cooked over the fireplace.

Katie felt overwhelmed by all that she was expected to do. It seemed that Helena was always crying or wanting to be held. The minute she picked the baby up, Helena would grab at her necklace. Katie would have to balance the baby on her hip while she leaned over the hot fire to stir the samp in the kettle. This porridge-like mush wasn't very appetizing. Little Jan and Christina liked to play near the fire but sometimes got too close. Katie found she had to watch them all of the time to keep them safe.

What a relief it was when Helena finally became sleepy, and allowed Katie to put her in the wooden cradle near the fireplace. Jan and Christina were happily playing on the floor with a pot and wooden spoon that Katie had given them. Now she was faced with the task of baking bread, which Mevrouw Van Vorst said needed to be done today. When Katie had asked for a recipe, Mevrouw Van Vorst had smiled in a puzzled way and said, "Just do it as it is done where you are from, child."

Katie tried hard to remember last Christmas, when she had finally agreed to help Anna bake bread for the holiday. Thinking back to the safety and comforts of her home she realized how much she missed her family, even Anna.

Searching around through barrels and bins where food supplies were kept, Katie gathered the ingredients she thought would make good bread. She looked around for measuring cups but couldn't find any. So she just mixed everything together in a big wooden bowl and was very relieved when the mixture became a gooey ball. Katie mixed in a little more flour, kneaded it a few times, and then put it back in the bowl on the hearth to rise.

"There! That wasn't so hard," she said to herself. She was beginning to feel a little better about all of this!

Waiting for the dough to rise, Katie turned her attention to what was going on around her. Jan and Christina were still busy on the floor, and Helena was asleep in her cradle. Katie could hear the sound of someone chopping wood. Coming from the back of the house, there were also the sounds of animals nearby. Katie thought she heard the clucking of chickens and a funny grunting sound that may have been pigs. The loudest noise was definitely an unhappy cow.

Katie realized that she had been hearing its bellowing all morning. Now it was even louder. Just at that moment, Cornelius came stomping in from the tavern.

"Has the cow not been milked yet?" he asked her in an angry voice.

"I don't know how to milk a cow!" she replied, surprised and a little annoyed.

"What is wrong with you? You must be stupid, you lazy girl. Go tend to the cow. It is part of your job!"

Katie felt her cheeks grow hot. Tears filled her eyes. *I've worked so hard this morning,* she thought angrily. Overwhelmed, but knowing that she had to continue to act like a servant, she opened the door to the back room, where she was amazed to find herself face to face with a large, tan colored cow. Several very fat pigs rushed at her, looking for food. The smell, a mixture of hay and manure, made her cover her nose with her hand. As she looked at the huge restless cow, its deep rumbling moos filled the small space. Just as she realized that there was no way she was going to go any closer to that cow, much less milk it, the door opened and Pieter stepped into the room.

"Why have you not milked the cow?" he asked, pushing the hungry pigs away.

Seeing her chance, Katie put on her sweetest smile and said, "I'll bet you are really good at milking."

"I am, but it is your job," Pieter said matter-of-factly.

Thinking fast, Katie reached into the pocket tied at her waist and took out some bubble gum she had been saving. Making sure Pieter was watching, she unwrapped one piece and stuck it in her mouth. Pieter watched her with wide eyes.

As she chewed the gum slowly, she asked, "Why are these smelly animals in the house?"

Pieter's eyes never left Katie's mouth. "Where else would we keep them? It is very cold outside. What are you doing?" he exclaimed as she blew a large pink bubble.

Taking her time, Katie popped the bubble and pulled another piece of gum from her pocket. "It's gum," Katie answered. Pieter looked puzzled. "You know, like candy... it's sweet. Do you want to try it?" she asked innocently.

Pieter hesitated, but only for a second. He nodded and reached for the gum, as Katie quickly hid it behind her back.

"I'll give it to you if you do something for me. You milk that cow and I'll give you this gum." Katie blew another bubble that burst with a loud pop. Nodding his agreement, Pieter quickly grabbed a wooden bucket and began to milk the cow. In no time he finished the job and gave the cow a friendly pat. He turned to Katie expectantly. With a relieved smile, she handed him the gum.

Just then Cornelius strode into the room. "What is going on here? Pieter, have you collected the eggs? Katje, Helena is crying again! Must I always tell you what to do?" He turned angrily and left.

Picking up the heavy milk bucket, Katie trudged back to the crying Helena. Checking quickly on Jan and Christina, she was horrified to find both of them covered with gooey bread dough. They had found the bowl that Katie had set to rise on the hearth!

Not knowing what to do first, Katie picked up the screaming Helena and tried bouncing her up and down.

Helena stopped crying as she grabbed for Katie's button necklace and tried to put it in her mouth. Looking around for something to give to Helena to keep her happy for a few minutes, Katie saw some gourds hanging from the ceiling beams. She knew that the dried seeds inside would make a rattling noise. With Helena balanced on one hip, Katie reached up and took down the smallest gourd. It rattled just as she had hoped. Immediately losing interest in the button, Helena reached for this new plaything, and Katie quickly slipped the button safely inside her blouse. Now she had to deal with Christina and Jan, who were still happily playing in the bread dough. She was relieved that Helena was willing to be put down in her cradle with the rattle. In her best grown-up voice, Katie called to Christina firmly, "You've been naughty! You and Jan have made a mess out of the bread dough. Now what am I going to do?" Christina's big blue eyes filled with tears and Katie almost felt sorry for her, but in her mind she could hear Cornelius criticizing her again. This was going to make it even harder for her to prepare the noon meal. She grabbed the bowl of dough from Christina and Jan, placing it on the table out of their reach. Turning back to the children, she picked off as much of the gooey dough as she could from their hands and clothing. Plopping the gray dough scraps back into the bowl, Katie took hot water from the kettle on the fireplace and mixed it with some cold water from a bucket on the floor. She quickly wiped the children's sticky hands and faces. Just then the outside door scraped open, and Pieter returned carrying two heavy buckets filled with water.

"Guess what I just heard out in the tavern?" he said excitedly.

It took Katie a moment to realize that Pieter was talking about the business that Mevrouw VanVorst ran in their front room.

Before Katie could reply, Pieter rushed on, "The men out front say that perhaps the French with their Indian friends will attack soon! It is a good thing we have the English soldiers garrisoned here in our town."

Katie's heart sank as she remembered that the English soldiers had not been able to stop the attack.

Pieter rushed on breathlessly. "The men are arguing about the need to do something to prepare. Myndert Wemp says he thinks there will be no attack because there is the feel of snow in the air. For the French to attack, it would mean a long march from Montreal. That would be very hard, even for our enemies." Trying to sound important, Pieter added, "I think they should place guards at the north and south gates just to be sure."

Hearing of the coming snow and the guards at the gates, Katie was reminded of Lawrence's last words:

When the snow covers the moon,
Your heart will see clearly,
The gateway to the past is the door to the future.

Maybe he's talking about the night of the massacre, Katie thought anxiously. *Is the door to the future how I get home? Does it have something to do with one of the gates?*

Katie was sure she was on the right track when she felt the necklace become warm once again. But the knowledge of what was to come sent chills up her spine.

THE BROKEN CHAIN

Katie was awakened by noises coming from below as Mevrouw Van Vorst readied the fire for the day. Lying on the uncomfortable straw mattress, she thought about what a disaster yesterday had been. The family had been polite, but no one would touch the bread that had turned out to be gray and rubbery on the inside and charred on the outside. It seemed as if everything she was expected to do as a servant ended up in a mess. Cornelius had spent the whole day yelling at her, and even Mevrouw Van Vorst, who tried to be kind at first, became impatient.

Katie's thoughts wandered back to Lawrence's puzzling words.

"...When the snow covers the moon..." That was it! A big blizzard *did* happen on the night of the Massacre! There was also something about a gate...she had to get to a gate when it started to snow. But which gate did Lawrence mean?

Maybe I should just go back to the gate that I came through with Lawrence, she thought. As if in agreement, the button burned against her chest. Katie took the button in her hand and in a frightened voice she whispered, "What kind of power do you have?"

But there was no more time for thinking. Katie heard heavy footsteps climbing the ladder to her garret. Cornelius's voice called angrily to her, "Why is our servant not up? The fire has been made and the morning meal is already prepared. You must come down now. We can wait no longer!" Startled, Katie threw off the comforter and leapt onto the cold floor. *If...no, WHEN I get home, I'm not going to complain about the things that Dad and Anna ask me to do,* she thought as she fought back tears.

Katie had no sooner scrambled down the ladder, when she found herself busy with the day's chores. After everybody had finished their morning meal and had gone off to do their own jobs, Katie found herself alone with the small children. Helena was crying again as usual, wanting to be picked up. Katie gave Jan and Christina the pot and wooden spoons to occupy them, since it had worked yesterday. As she bent over Helena's cradle, the baby's hand reached out to grab at the button. A strong yank from Helena's pudgy hand finally broke the delicate chain.

"Oh no!" Katie gasped. She knew that somehow she needed the button to get home. Using the gourd rattle to distract Helena, she was able to pry the necklace out of the baby's hand. "I'd better find someplace safe to put this," Katie said.

Her eyes swept the room looking for a likely hiding place. On the wooden dresser was a pewter tankard that Katie thought might be just the right spot. With Helena on her hip, she crossed the room and carefully slipped the necklace under the covered top of the tankard. But putting the necklace in the tankard made her feel sad. Her family had given her that button and chain. She missed them so much. She HAD to find a way home. She was so deep in her own thoughts that she didn't see Pieter slip silently out of the room. He had been watching her the whole time.

SOUP FOR A NEIGHBOR

Mevrouw Van Vorst's voice interrupted Katie's thoughts. "Fetch your cloak, child, Mevrouw Potman has been gravely ill with the fever. You must take this kettle of soup to her."

Thankful for a chance to leave the kitchen, and hoping she might find Lawrence, Katie grabbed the heavy kettle and went out through the Dutch door. Standing on the front stoop, she blinked in the bright daylight. It felt good to be out of the dark, cramped house. A brisk February wind whipped her cloak around her. Following the directions that Mevrouw Van Vorst had given, Katie set out towards the nearby corner where the Potman family lived. Her eyes searched constantly for any sign of Lawrence the Indian.

As Katie approached the stoop of the Potman house, she noticed that it looked similar to all the others: its gabled end faced the street, and it was a mix of clapboard and brick. Katie stepped up on to the stoop and rapped on the door. A gruff- looking man opened the door.

"Who are you?" he said sharply.

"I'm living with Mevrouw Van Vorst," Katie answered, "and she wanted your wife to have this soup."

"Oh! You are the new servant girl. Well, do not just stand there! Come and put the kettle on the hearth!"

As Katie's eyes adjusted to the dim light inside, she could see that this house had only one room. Katie was surprised that Mevrouw Potman was nowhere in sight. Then she heard a weak cough from behind a curtain, which covered the built-in bed.

"I hope your wife will be feeling better soon, Mijnheer Potman," Katie said politely.

He nodded quickly, but then pointed to Katie's feet. In an annoyed tone, he said, "Watch your feet, girl, you are tracking mud all over the floor!"

"I'm sorry," Katie murmured as she moved toward the door. "Boy, what a grouch!" she muttered as the door closed behind her.

Katie knew she should go right back to help Mevrouw Van Vorst, but it felt good to be outside. Besides, she needed time to think about how she was going to get home. She paused just a moment in front of the Potmans, and then kept walking. Maybe she could find that gate Lawrence spoke of in his message.

As she walked, she came to the cross street. She stopped and looked first to her right and then to her left. She saw with dismay that there seemed to be big wooden gates at both ends of the street. *Which gate did he mean? How will I know?* Katie's hand went to the place around her neck where the button usually lay. With a jolt she remembered that she had put it in the tankard. Maybe it had been a mistake to leave it behind.

She seemed to need the button to know what to do. With a last glance at the gates, Katie was about to turn back when she saw a familiar figure in the distance. She recognized at once the proud silhouette of Lawrence astride his horse. Without a moment's thought she started running towards him. "Wait!" she shouted.

But it was already too late. Lawrence had disappeared. Breathlessly, she arrived at the North gate. Tears of frustration filled her eyes. "He didn't wait for me. Where did he go?" Standing in the open gateway, Katie brushed away the tears. Not wanting to leave the safety of the stockade walls, her eyes searched in every direction for any sign of Lawrence. But there was no evidence that anyone had even been there. The fresh snow that had fallen during the night was undisturbed. Not one hoof print marred the new white blanket. *I know that I saw him. It had to be Lawrence!* But nothing could totally surprise her anymore after what she had been through for the last three days.

Katie forced herself to take a few deep breaths to calm down. Carefully looking around, she searched for something that was familiar. Was this the gate that she had come through with Lawrence? The sound of crunching footsteps on the snow behind her caused her to whirl around, hoping to see Lawrence. But instead, the short, stocky figure of a man approached.

"Goeden morgan," he called as he got closer.

Katie felt a flash of recognition. This man had been one of the watchmen on that confusing first day when she had arrived with Lawrence. So this must be the gate where she had entered. "Did you see Lawrence the Mohawk? He was just here," Katie asked hopefully.

"No, no one has been through here since last night," said the watchman kindly. "Does Mevrouw Van Vorst know you are here?"

"Well, she sent me on an errand, but don't worry, I'm going back now." With that, she turned and made her way towards the tavern. Katie said the words calmly, but time was running out. Would she be able to find Lawrence before the massacre started?

FIRE!

The scene that greeted Katie when she walked in the door was a familiar one by now. Jan and Christina were playing happily on the floor near the hearth. Christina held a small cloth "doll" made from a knotted linen table napkin. Jan squealed with delight as she pretended to dance the doll around him. Helena, who was lying on her stomach, began to rock on her knees. To everyone's amazement, she haltingly began to crawl towards the doll.

"Look, Mother! Helena is crawling!" called Pieter excitedly.

Mevrouw Van Vorst paused as she ladled steaming soup into bowls at the hot hearth. She wiped her brow and said, "That is good, but it will mean that Helena will not want to stay in her cradle anymore."

"Katje, you will need to watch her even more closely," Cornelius ordered in his usual commanding tone of voice.

"Great," Katie muttered under her breath, "that's all I need right now."

The midday meal was over quickly. Everybody rushed off to do their never-ending chores, leaving Katie to clean up and watch over the younger children. As soon as she was alone she went to the tankard to get her button. Reaching inside, her fingers felt around for it, but it was not there! She turned the tankard upside down and out fell the broken chain, but no button.

The tankard fell from her hands. With a loud clatter it hit the floor. All of the tears of frustration and fear that she had been holding inside broke loose and she sank to the floor, sobbing.

In a moment she felt a pair of strong arms slip around her. "You poor child, what is it that has upset you so?" she heard Mevrouw Van Vorst ask. Katie felt herself move into those comforting arms. Her sobbing quieted as Mevrouw Van Vorst gently stroked her hair. It had been a long time since Katie had allowed herself to be comforted by anyone, although Anna had often tried. She realized, as she snuggled into those motherly arms encircling her, that her tears were for more than just the button. She was so frightened. She was so homesick ...and she would give anything to see her own mother, even just one more time. She lifted her tear-stained face to look up into the woman's gentle blue eyes. "You are new to us right now," Mevrouw Van Vorst was saying, "but soon you will come to know that we can be your friends." Her warm smile reminded Katie of Anna's. Katie knew that she could trust this kind woman.

"My button is missing!" Katie blurted out. I put it in the tankard so it would be safe...and now it's gone. I have to get my button back! I need it to get home. I know something terrible is going to happen. None of us are safe here."

In a soothing voice, Mevrouw Van Vorst said, "We will find your button. I know it was from your father and it is important to you."

"No," Katie cried, "You don't understand! There's going to be a massacre and we could all be killed!"

"Ah, I see Pieter has been talking to you," said Mevrouw Van Vorst calmly. "We hear all kinds of tales in the tavern. Pay them no mind, Katje."

Standing and smoothing her rumpled apron, Mevrouw Van Vorst said firmly, "I must go and tend to Mevrouw Potman. Her husband has asked me to come look in on her. I will speak to the boys about your button later." As she flung her cloak over her shoulders, Mevrouw Van Vorst glanced at the children playing on the floor. "Katje, you must remember to watch Helena closely now that she is crawling."

Katie followed her into the narrow hallway, hoping to convince her of the coming danger. But as she watched Mevrouw Van Vorst disappear through the doorway she knew that no one was going to believe her. She shivered as a blast of cold February air chilled the hallway. What could she do now?

Lost in thought, Katie headed back towards the warmth of the fireplace. It was unusually quiet as she stepped back into the room. That could only mean one thing! She remembered what a mess the children had made with the bread dough on her first day. They probably were up to something right now. She relaxed a little when she peeked over the back of the settle and saw Jan, Christina and Helena sound asleep on the floor, snuggled together like a pile of exhausted puppies. In spite of herself, she had to admit they were cute. Glancing at the wood box, she sighed, realizing that they needed more wood. "Furnaces were sure a great invention," she grumbled as she hurried outside to the woodpile before the children woke up from their nap.

As she came back through the doorway with an armload of wood, her thoughts were on her lost button. But the smell of something burning snapped her back to the present. Sniffing the air, she looked around with alarm to see what was on fire. Instantly she saw what had happened.

In the short time that Helena had been left alone, she had managed to unwind the layers of cloth in which she was bundled. Finding herself free to crawl, she made a beeline for the hearth with a long tail of cloth dragging behind her. The fire was too hot, and Helena had turned away to explore a different spot. As she turned, the end of the cloth swept over some glowing embers that had fallen on the hearth. Now, Katie watched in horror as the smoldering end of the cloth suddenly burst into flames before her eyes.

Katie dropped her armload of wood, grabbed her woolen cloak from the peg by the door, and rushed toward Helena, shouting for help. Hoping to smother the fire, she dropped the cloak over the flames, which were now just inches from the frightened baby. As Katie was beating at the flames, Cornelius rushed in from the tavern. Flinging the cloak aside, he grabbed the leather fire bucket, which was on the hearth, and dumped water on the smoky mess. Katie scooped Helena into her arms and hugged her tightly as she tried to calm the screaming child. Turning to Cornelius with tears in her eyes, Katie struggled to keep her voice steady.

"It was my fault. I know I shouldn't have left them, even for a minute. I'm so sorry, Cornelius."

To her surprise, Cornelius said in a kinder voice than usual, "You were very brave, Katje. You saved Helena's life."

Later in the evening, Katie sat with the family around the hearth as the fire crackled. The dim light in the room came from the fire and danced on the blue and white tiles that framed the fireplace. In the flickering light, Cornelius and Pieter sat on low stools playing checkers. The younger children were already sound asleep in the trundle that had been pulled from under the large, built-in bed. The click of Mevrouw Van Vorst's wooden knitting needles sent Katie's thoughts back to Anna. Katie was surprised to find herself thinking of her step-mother. Anna had spent many nights knitting her a beautiful woolen sweater in Katie's favorite shade of green. With a flush of regret, Katie remembered how she had purposely never worn it. She wished that Anna were here right now. There were so many things she would like to say to her.

The soothing rhythm of the knitting needles stopped as Mevrouw Van Vorst rose from her seat to check on Helena who was tucked safely in her cradle by the fire. "Katje, it is time to take the coals from the fire and put them in the warming pans," she said. The warming pans would be put in the beds to take away the chill. Katie had been told to do this as part of her chores. "When you are done, come back to the fire and we will talk." When Katie returned to the fire, she found that the checker game was over and Mevrouw Van Vorst had passed around steaming tankards of hot cider. Handing one to Katie, she smiled and said, "We are so thankful that your quick thinking saved Helena this afternoon."

Katie blushed at this praise, since she still felt guilty about leaving the children alone even for just a few minutes. Mevrouw Van Vorst turned to her sons. "Katje tells me she has lost her gold button."

"I didn't lose it!" interrupted Katie, "I put it in the tan-kard on the dresser when Helena broke the chain and now it's gone!"

Cornelius looked at her blankly, but Pieter's eyes would not meet hers. He shifted nervously on the stool and looked down at his feet.

"Pieter, do you know anything about this?" asked Mev-rouw Van Vorst sharply. Pieter, shook his head no, but would not meet his mother's gaze. Katie felt her heart sink as she saw her chances of returning home slipping away.

An uncomfortable silence filled the room until Mev-rouw Van Vorst said, "I feel there is more to this story than is being told, but I fear there is no more we can do about it tonight." She paused and looked at Katie. "Katje, I have thought much of a fitting reward for your bravery. I think I know what I will do."

With that, she lit a tallow candle and went to the dresser along the wall. In the dim light Katie could not see what was in Mevrouw Van Vorst's hand as she returned. Opening a small, carved box, she took something out and held it in her hand. Speaking softly, she stepped closer to Katie and said, "Today you have saved something that is very precious to us, but you have lost something that is precious to you. I want you to have this, even though I know it cannot replace the one your father gave to you."

She opened her hand. There, in the light of the fire, glinted another button, which to Katie's amazement looked just like hers! Seeing Katie's surprise, Mevrouw Van Vorst was quick to say, "Just like your button, child, this one was given to me by my mother who is dead these many years."

Katie clutched the button in her hand. Tears filled her eyes as she smiled gratefully at this family that was beginning to treat her as one of their own. "I will treasure this always," she said in a hushed voice.

Rising from her seat by the fire, Katie hugged Mevrouw Van Vorst warmly and smiled shyly at Pieter and Cornelius.

"And now," Mevrouw Van Vorst announced, "it has been an eventful day and it is time for us all to be in our beds!"

Later, curled under the warm comforter in the garret, Katie lay wide awake, on her lumpy straw mattress, thinking about what she should do next. *I've tried to warn them,* she thought, *but they just don't believe me. I've tried to find Lawrence. I can't pretend to be this servant Katje much longer or I'm going to be trapped here when the massacre happens.*

Crying softly, so that she would not awaken Pieter and Cornelius, who were sleeping on the other mattress, Katie reached for the new button Mevrouw Van Vorst had given her. She had replaced the broken chain, with a snippet of yarn from Mevrouw's knitting. It seemed cool to her touch. Would this button have the same power as the other one? She lay still, holding the button tightly, hoping to feel the familiar warmth. Downstairs the door latch rattled as the night watchman made his hourly rounds, reassuring everyone that all was safe. But Katie knew that wasn't true. She knew they weren't safe at all!

AN APOLOGY

This seems like a mild day for February, Katie thought as she swept the stoop in front of the tavern. She could hear the steady dripping of water off the thatched roof. Slush filled the muddy roads, making it hard to travel even a short distance. At any other time, Katie might have enjoyed the bright, warm sun but today all she could think about was the massacre. Her eyes searched for Lawrence.

The tavern door swung open and a group of men brushed past her. They were so involved in their heated discussion that they never noticed her.

"The wars between the English and the French rulers for control of these lands have little to do with me!" one of the men grumbled. "I just wish to earn my living and raise my family. If I want to trade for a few furs now and then, it should be no one's business but my own."

"They say two thousand French are on their way from Montreal to attack our village. We must be prepared to protect ourselves!" said a stout, red-faced man. "While the Iroquois who live near us are our friends, we will need to be wary of those who live near the French and have taken up their side."

He was rudely interrupted by a taller man wearing a leather apron. "You are a fool, Mijnheer Aukes! That is the very reason Lieutenant Talmadge, and his garrison from Connecticut are here. With those soldiers here, we have nothing to fear from the French."

"I do not worry half as much about the French as I do about the laws made in Albany that forbid us from trading with our Mohawk neighbors," said a fourth deep-voiced man, who wore the traditional knee breeches and buckled shoes.

The men moved down the street and continued their loud discussion, but Katie's attention was diverted to Cornelius, who was making his way toward her through the slush. As he approached, Katie noticed that he had a pair of ice skates slung over his shoulder on a leather strap. Their carved wooden blades bumped against his back with each step.

"Ach! The river is no good for skating. This thaw has caused too much slush," Cornelius complained when he saw her. He continued on into the tavern, but Katie's heart sank. She remembered that, according to what she had learned in school, there had been a thaw just before the massacre. "I have to do something NOW," she resolved.

She turned and followed Cornelius into the dimly lit tavern. A jumble of questions flooded her mind. Where was the button her father had given her? Could she get home without it? How could she get out by herself to continue her search for Lawrence? Cornelius was always watching her. With new determination, she decided to talk to him and make up a reason for leaving the house.

Just as Katie was about to approach him, a call for more beer came from two men who were sitting at the wooden table near the fireplace. They were talking excitedly. Finding the keg almost empty, Cornelius began the task of putting a tap in a new keg while calling over his shoulder to Katie, "The fire is getting too low, Katje, put more wood on it!"

Determined to talk to Cornelius, Katie hung her cloak on the pegs near the door and shoved the broom she had been using into the corner. Passing the men on her way to the fireplace, Katie could hear their conversation. In a weary tone of voice, the first man said, "The fight over who is going to control these lands seems to have no end. I was there when we marched with the Iroquois to Canada and burned the French city of LaChine. Ach! It was a bloody time! The whole town was burned--and over three hundred of their people were killed."

"I have long feared we would pay the price for that attack," said the second man. "It is only a matter of time before the governor of Canada sends a raiding party for revenge."

The first man laughed grimly. "We won't have to worry about that tonight. Did you see the sky when we came in? The winds are blowing in from the north--that means a blizzard for sure!"

Katie remembered there had been a blizzard after the thaw the night of the massacre. It was all happening exactly as she had learned in school! She brushed past Pieter, who was scooping ashes out of the fireplace and shoveling them into an ash bucket. Seconds later, as she bent down to pick up a load of firewood, Katie was startled by a loud crash. She turned to see the ash bucket overturned and Pieter standing there with a dismayed look on his face. The empty bucket rolled under a table as a cloud of powdery ashes rose into the air. Several patrons scrambled from their seats, cursing loudly. The boy's red face became pale when he saw an angry Cornelius stomping towards him. Pieter glanced quickly at Katie, his eyes silently pleading for help. Katie found herself feeling sorry for the trembling boy. She knew all too well how Cornelius' anger felt.

"You clumsy fool! Look what you have done," shouted Cornelius.

"I-I-I'm sorry, Cornelius...I don't know what happened! It just slipped."

Something snapped inside Katie. Servant or not, she had had enough of Cornelius' bullying.

"Leave him alone! It was an accident!" Katie heard her own voice sounding very loud and angry.

Cornelius glanced around. All conversation had stopped in the tavern. The patrons were watching to see what would happen next. Cornelius stared at Katie in amazement, clearly not expecting a servant to speak to him this way.

"We will discuss this later," he said in an angry but controlled voice. "Both of you will clean up this mess and put some wood on the fire."

Turning on his heel, Cornelius marched out of the room with his head held high. Pieter breathed a huge sigh of relief. Katie was too upset to notice his smile of gratitude, because she knew that now Cornelius would never listen to her..

A short time later, Katie and Pieter finished their work. A merry fire crackled at the hearth and the wide-planked wooden floor had been swept clean once again. Pieter watched with relief as the morning's last customer finally left. From across the room, Katie saw him beckoning from where he stood by the fireplace.

"Come here, Katje, there is something you should see."

Curious, Katie walked over to him. She watched as he carefully jiggled a loose brick from the wall of the fireplace, and pulled it out, revealing a small hiding place. Katie leaned forward and peered into the dark hole.

"What's this?" Katie asked as she reached in and pulled out a small, round, glittering object. She could feel the heat of it in her hand even before Pieter answered.

"I hope you will forgive me. I was wrong to take what did not belong to me," whispered Pieter.

With a flood of relief, Katie realized with the button now in her hand, there was a chance she could get back home. The huge smile on her face told Pieter he was forgiven.

THE PLAN

Katie could tell from the darkening sky that it was growing late in the afternoon. She also knew the blizzard was coming; she could feel the dampness in the air. With increasing desperation she devised a plan that would get her out of the house and give her time to search for Lawrence. Knowing there was no time to waste, Katie slipped the button Mevrouw Van Vorst had given her from around her neck. With shaky fingers, she untied the knot in the yarn. She took the button her father had given her from her pocket, and compared the two. They really were identical!

Katie closed her fist tightly around the two buttons and brought them close to her heart. Choking back a sob that caught at her throat, she whispered hoarsely, "Please, oh please let my plan work…and please keep Mevrouw Van Vorst and this family safe, too!" A familiar warmth inside her closed fist made her quickly slip her own button onto the yarn and slide the second button into her pocket. The next part of her plan would be difficult.

She knew she shouldn't lie, but she felt she had no other choice. Katie went to find Mevrouw Van Vorst, who was busy weaving dark blue woolen cloth on the loom. Feeling very guilty about what she was going to do, Katie took a deep breath and said, "Mijnheer Potman just stopped by. He said to tell you that his wife is a little better today. She would like you to send her some more soup. I would be happy to take it to her."

Nodding her head, Mevrouw Van Vorst rose from the loom. "Very well," she said. "I have a pot on the fire right now. I will send one of my healing tonics as well."

Katie bent and picked up Helena. Rocking the baby gently in her lap, Katie went over and over Lawrence's last words:

The gateway to the past is the door to the future.

She thought she had come into the past with Lawrence through the North gate. Maybe that was her gateway to the past? And if the gateway to the past is the door to the future, could he mean her future? Maybe that was where she had to go in order to get home. After all, what these people call the future is where she had come from.

A short time later Katie found herself outside with the tankard of hot tonic, and a small pot of soup, supposedly on her way to the Potman's home. She had not gone very far when a commotion caught her attention. Across the street, at the corner house, a Dutch woman was shouting angrily at a Native American woman. From what Katie remembered about Schenectady history, she guessed the woman was a Mohawk. The Dutch woman was waving her broom in a threatening way and pointing at the other woman's muddy, wet feet. Katie watched as the Mohawk woman seemed to give up, shrugged, turned away, and strode off into the swirling flakes that had now begun to fall. With alarm, Katie realized that even though she was too far away to hear the words the two women had exchanged, she knew their story all too well. She had grown up hearing the legend of a friendly Native American woman who went to Dominie Tessemaker's house and tried to warn the Dutch settlers about the attack planned by the French.

She knew that the Mohawk woman never had the chance to deliver her warning because she had tracked mud onto Dominie Tessemaker's clean floor and had been chased out of the house before she could speak. Now, as the woman brushed angrily past Katie, their eyes met and Katie was struck by how much those dark flashing eyes reminded her of her friend, Nikki. Sometimes when Katie and Nikki disagreed, Katie saw that same determined look in Nikki's dark eyes as she struggled to control her temper.

Katie shook her head and turned away. It was frightening how her life and her future had become so entangled with the past!

After going down the road safely out of sight from the tavern, Katie looked for a likely place to get rid of the tankard and soup pot. She was sorry, but she had no intention of going to the Potman's house this time. She had a different plan.

Katie walked quickly. She passed the Potman house and found the path that ran along the stockade fence. She was hopeful that this path might lead her to the North gate. She wished she had a map. But wait! Digging in the pocket tied at her waist, her fingers closed around the crumpled map that Nikki had given her at the Schenectady celebration. It seemed like forever ago. The map confirmed that she could reach the gate from here. But would she find Lawrence?

The snow was falling more rapidly. It seemed even darker as evening approached because the moon was hidden behind thick snow clouds. Shivering with both cold and fear, Katie pulled the cloak around herself more tightly.

Her hands had been clutching the cloak to her neck. Now, through the heavy layers of cloth, she could feel the growing warmth of her button, which once again hung around her neck on the snippet of yarn.

For the first time all day, Katie felt hopeful. She was sure that the button was guiding her, and this gave her courage. *If only I can find Lawrence*, thought Katie. *I miss my family, even Gerritt. I wish I could have a second chance to make things better with Anna. There are so many things I would change, if only I could get back home.*

By now she had reached the corner of the stockade. The path she was following turned left towards a wooden watchtower that was part of the stockade wall. The northeasterly wind whipped the wet snow against her and she hunched against the bitter cold. The smell of freshly cut pine from woodpiles mingled with the smoky, wood burning smell that hung heavily over the settlement. Any other time she would have enjoyed these rich outdoor smells, which reminded her of Adirondack ski trips with her family. But, tonight, all she could think about was finding Lawrence.

The North gate was in sight, and Katie's steps quickened almost to a run. As she approached the gate, her heart was pounding. She could feel the hot button against her chest; it seemed to be getting even hotter. Squinting, her eyes searched through the dense flakes. She was startled by the sudden appearance of a figure on a horse ahead of her near the gate. Her fear of horses was pushed aside by the possibility that this was finally Lawrence. She ran towards him. It was Lawrence!

Shouting as she ran, Katie pleaded, "Please, please don't leave me again. I need to get home tonight!"

Lawrence gazed steadily at her. He said nothing, but seemed to be waiting for something more.

"Lawrence," she panted, "you brought me here, so you must be able to get me home! I know that terrible things are going to happen here tonight—you probably know too!" Afraid he would disappear again, she grabbed his deerskin-covered leg. Her sudden movement startled the horse, causing it to sidestep. But Katie didn't even notice.

"Why don't you say something, Lawrence? How can I make you understand?" she demanded. She looked steadily at him and spoke slowly, never taking her eyes from his face. "My heart does see clearly now. I know what could happen to me if I stay here much longer—but it's not only that! Living with Mevrouw Van Vorst has taught me a lot about loving my own family. I know it was wrong of me to not give Anna a chance. She and Dad will never know how much I love them if I don't get back home." By now Katie was crying in spite of herself. Her warm tears melted the snow as it fell against her face.

Finally Lawrence spoke. "You have learned well," he said gently.

Flooded with relief, Katie understood that he was going to help her.

HELP FROM LAWRENCE

Leaning forward slightly, Lawrence held out his strong arm to help swing Katie up behind him on the horse. Katie reached for his outstretched hand. She was going home! Soon she would be back safely with her own family. But wait…if she left right now, what would happen to Mevrouw Van Vorst and her family? She stepped back. "I can't go with you now. I have to try to save Mevrouw Van Vorst and her family."

Lawrence nodded. Looking into his eyes, Katie could see that he understood.

"But how will I find you again?" asked Katie. As if to answer her, Lawrence slid off the horse and handed Katie the braided leather reins. "You mean your horse will lead me back to you?" Katie asked. Once again, Lawrence nodded.

Katie looked at the horse and at her own shaking hand holding the reins. Up until this moment she had been too caught up in her excitement about finding Lawrence to think about anything else. Now her fear of horses crowded in on her. She felt as if she couldn't breathe; her whole body was trembling. Every inch of her just wanted to run away.

No, she said firmly to herself. *I have to do this. The only chance I have of ever getting home is to trust this horse.* She tried to calm down and think more clearly. She grasped the reins more firmly and tugged the horse's head around in her direction. The horse gazed at her calmly, and Katie felt a little more optimistic. *I can do this*, she told herself again, and as if in agreement, the horse nudged her gently with his soft, velvety nose.

Turning to assure Lawrence that she would return as soon as she could, Katie found that once again he had disappeared. "Well, I guess we're on our own," she said to the horse with a sigh.

A movement off to her right caught her attention. Just outside the North gate, the two watchmen were standing guard. The snow was falling heavily now, and the men looked skyward with growing concern. *Oh, the legend must not be true!* thought Katie, *"I always heard they left snowmen guarding the gates because they didn't think there really would be an attack. I wish I could get them to take the threat of an attack more seriously. Maybe things would work out differently. I have to try to warn them.* The watchmen didn't pay any attention to Katie as she led the horse down the rutted path towards them. Sounding braver than she felt, Katie called out to them.

"Please listen to me! There's going to be a massacre here tonight!"

Startled, the men turned towards Katie's voice. They recognized her at once. "Why, it's the servant girl from Mevrouw Van Vorst's tavern!" said one man to the other.

"Who has heard too many stories at the tavern," added the second man, laughingly.

Raising his eyes to the falling snow again, the first man agreed. "There would never be an attack on a night like this." Sadly, Katie knew she could not make them believe her. Turning away, she continued on the path to the tavern with the hope that at least Mevrouw Van Vorst might still be convinced. If Katie had any doubt about whether she had made the right decision, it disappeared when she felt the warmth of the glowing button against her skin.

THE COIN

Katie moved slowly as she led the horse through the deepening snow towards Mevrouw Van Vorst's house. Her pace quickened as the house came into sight. Instinctively knowing the horse would not leave, Katie dropped the reins, ran up onto the stoop, and burst into the tavern. The front room was empty because of the approaching storm. "Where is everyone?" Katie called. "Mevrouw Van Vorst, where are you?" She turned and ran down the narrow hallway back to the family's living quarters, where everyone looked at her with curiosity as she rushed breathlessly in.

Touching her arm, Mevrouw Van Vorst said, "Calm yourself, child. What is it that has you so upset?"

Katie's words tumbled in a rush. "You have to leave here right now! The settlement is going to be attacked! There's going to be a massacre! I know for a fact that your whole family could be killed. You've got to believe me!"

Mevrouw Van Vorst turned away with a gentle smile. "Ah, we've talked about this before. You cannot believe all of the things that are heard out in the tavern. You must calm yourself, Katje, there is still much work to be done. Please add some wood to the fire and ready the bowls for our meal. Pieter, go and bring in more firewood. Katje, when you have finished with the bowls, come and watch the little ones so that I can finish with my work."

But Katie grabbed Mevrouw Van Vorst's arm. "You don't understand. Please believe me. I know this because… because…I'm from the future!"

A look of disbelief crossed Mevrouw Van Vorst's face, but Katie rushed on. "I'm not who you think I am! I can't explain how I got here, but I'm really from another time!"

Concern replaced the disbelief in Mevrouw Van Vorst's eyes. She put her hand on Katie's forehead. "Could it be a fever that makes you speak of such odd things?"

"How can I prove to you that what I'm saying is true?" pleaded Katie. The button lying against her chest burned hotter and hotter. She looked around the room at the confused faces of this family she had come to care about, and knew she had to make them believe her somehow.

Dropping to her knees in front of Mevrouw Van Vorst, Katie sobbed, "I'm so frightened for all of us. I don't know what I can do to make you believe me." She slumped closer to the floor as she covered her face with her hands. A sudden sharp pain, caused by something round and hard under her right knee, gave her an idea.

Lifting the bottom of her long skirt, Katie's shaking fingers ripped frantically at its hem until she was able to pull out the silvery coin that Anna had lovingly sewn in for good luck.

"Look! Look at this coin!" Katie shouted, rising to her feet. "It's a coin from the year 1990!"

Taking the shiny coin from Katie's outstretched hand, Mevrouw Van Vorst and Pieter examined it suspiciously. "This is not like any coin we have ever seen," said Mevrouw Van Vorst with a frown.

"It's not like our Dutch guilders," agreed Pieter. "Who is this person? What are these numbers?"

With the button burning against her chest, Katie looked Mevrouw Van Vorst directly in the eye. "Look at it. It doesn't say 1690, it says 1990. The YEAR 1990! That's the year I come from!"

TO THE RIVER'S EDGE

For what seemed like a long time, Mevrouw Van Vorst studied the fear on Katie's face. She looked at each of her children; the little ones at play on the floor, Helena in her cradle, and Pieter, who was standing next to her, watching her intently. She looked back at the coin, still in her hand. Finally she spoke. "I do not know what to believe, Katje, but I know that you are convinced that a terrible thing will happen to us here tonight."

In a rush of relief, Katie let out the breath she had been holding. Mevrouw Van Vorst seemed to have made a decision.

"When Cornelius returns, we will make a plan. Katje, we will take your warning to heart. Perhaps nothing will come of it, but we will not take that chance."

Katie paced as she nervously fingered the button. The family had been worried about her when she had not returned from the Potmans, Mevrouw explained. Cornelius had insisted on going out to look for her because of the approaching storm. Now Katie worried that she had put the family in even greater danger. How long would they have to wait? If Cornelius had not had to look for her, they would be gone by now. The fact that the button was getting hotter as time went on convinced Katie that they had to act soon.

While they waited, Mevrouw Van Vorst insisted that the family sit and eat the evening meal that she had prepared. The children ate hungrily, but Katie, anxious to get everyone to safety, had trouble swallowing even a mouthful.

The time crept by slowly. "Where is Cornelius? What could be taking him so long?" Katie finally blurted out. No sooner had she spoken than they heard a door close and the sound of heavy footsteps coming down the long hallway. "Cornelius!" Katie cried in relief. Everyone rushed to him and began talking all at once.

Raising both hands to silence them, he turned to Katie and said, "I see you have returned to us safely, Katje. I saw you at the gate talking with Lawrence, the Mohawk. When you left him, you turned and walked toward home, so I knew you would be safe in the coming storm." Turning to his mother he continued, "Mijnheer Potman needed wood split and brought into the house before the snow deepened. I could not refuse to help."

Pieter, who had been hopping from one foot to the other in his great excitement, now burst out, "Katje says we all have to leave right away!"

Cornelius looked questioningly at Mevrouw Van Vorst. "Leave?" he said, and waited for an explanation.

"Cornelius," Mevrouw said slowly but firmly, "Katje has convinced me that we may be in danger if we stay in our home tonight. There is no time to argue. We will explain it all to you later."

Hearing the combination of fear and determination in his mother's voice, Cornelius knew that it would be of no use to ask any more questions. "All right, Mother," he said. He turned to Katie and said, "Katje, tell us what you know. When you spoke with Lawrence at the gate did he warn you of something?"

Katie thought quickly. How could she make him believe her? She needed more than just the coin. She stepped toward Cornelius and grabbed his arm. Looking directly at him Katie replied firmly, "Lawrence knows what is going to happen here tonight."

Cornelius stepped back, startled by Katie's boldness. For a moment he shared the fear he had heard in his mother's voice. But, quickly brushing that fear aside, he turned to Mevrouw Van Vorst and said, "Very well, Mother, I think we should prepare to leave, but where would we be safe?"

Katie remembered reading that Major John Glen and his home across the Mohawk River had been spared during the massacre. At Katie's urging, Mevrouw Van Vorst and Cornelius agreed that crossing the frozen river would be their only hope. Without wasting any time they busied themselves, gathering warm clothes and bundling up the children. It would be a difficult trek through the heavily falling snow. Mevrouw Van Vorst paused at the door. Her eyes swept across the room for one final look. She turned to Katie who was hurrying Jan and Christina along. "Katje, are you sure….?

The warmth of the button around her neck gave Katie the answer once again. "Yes," she said firmly, "We must leave now! We'd better hurry!"

Outside in the frigid night, Cornelius took control of the situation. "The youngest ones will ride. Katje, you will lead the horse."

"I can do that," Katie said, with a newly discovered confidence that took her by surprise. Cornelius went ahead of the little group, doing his best to stamp down a path in the knee-deep snow. Pieter followed, hunching his shoulders against the cold wind. Mevrouw struggled along next to Katie and the horse, cradling Helena against her body. Jan and Christina clung to each other atop the horse.

As they made their way slowly out of the North gate, towards the river, Katie couldn't keep herself from turning for one last glimpse of the sleeping settlement of Schoonechtendel. She knew that by morning's first light most of the people and their homes would be lost. As the cold and weary family reached the embankment along the river, frozen once again by the blizzard's icy wind, the button burned with an intense heat. Katie was sure it was hotter than it had ever been before. Standing at the edge of the river, Katie knew that across the few hundred feet of ice a safe place waited. If they were to survive the coming massacre, the family would need to reach the Glen home. If only she could go with them! Turning sadly towards Mevrouw Van Vorst, Katie was about to explain why she was not going with them across the river, but before she could speak, a blood-curdling scream pierced the snowy darkness. It was starting!

Cornelius turned to Katie with an incredulous look. "How did you know? How could you know what would happen?" he asked.

"It doesn't matter now," Katie said, and turned her attention to the children on the horse who were whimpering with fright. "Help me get them down."

As Pieter lifted Jan down to Katie, she looked into his frightened eyes and tried to smile reassuringly. Cornelius gathered Christina into his arms while the screams from the settlement grew louder. Suddenly, flames lit the sky and soon the air was thick with the smell of blazing thatch. Grasping the horse's reins tightly, Katie pleaded with Mevrouw Van Vorst. "You've got to hurry! You must cross the river NOW!"

"But what of you?" Mevrouw Van Vorst asked, shaking with fright. "Are you not coming with us?"

Tearfully Katie whispered, "If I am going back to my own time, I have to leave you. I need to find Lawrence, he's my only way home!"

It was their final goodbye, and they all knew it. Now, standing on the frozen riverbank, shivering in the cold, it was hard for them to part. Finally Mevrouw began speaking in a voice that shook with emotion. "Hopefully God will see fit to spare us. I do not know how it is that you have come to us, but we will never forget you, Katje. In our hearts you will always be a part of our family." For a moment, Mevrouw hugged Katie close, then after one last lingering look, the family turned toward the river and continued on. As the darkness gradually swallowed them, Katie forced herself to turn back alone towards the burning settlement.

THE MASSACRE

Leading the horse, Katie retraced their footsteps. It was difficult to walk as the horse lurched heavily behind her in the deep snow. Each step brought them closer to the billowing smoke that rose upward into the glowing pink sky. With each musket shot, Katie's dread increased. She was afraid of what awaited her if she didn't find Lawrence in time. As she approached the north gate, the pounding of her own heart seemed as loud as the shouts coming from inside the stockade. Sounds rushed at her: the high-pitched bawling of frightened livestock, the crackling tongues of flame licking at the wooden houses, the ear-splitting war cries that sent shivers down her spine. Katie could even hear the excited cursing of enemy French soldiers as some of the settlers fought furiously for their lives.

At the edge of the North gate the horse stopped abruptly, almost yanking Katie off her feet. Despite her desperate tugging on the reins, she could not get the horse to move another step. The noise of the massacre still raged on, but she could single out the sound of pounding hoof beats, which seemed to be coming right at her. She flinched as a musket shot rang out close by. The shot had found its target. A crouched rider, wounded in the leg, was clinging to the neck of his galloping horse as they flew past her. Another piece of history fell into place when Katie realized that this rider must be Symon Schermerhorn. She had grown up with the story of his brave, fifteen mile, ride that warned the people of Albany about a possible attack. Katie wished that right now she could be half as brave as he was.

A small group of fierce warriors charged out of the gate, determined to capture the wounded man. Seeing that Symon Schermerhorn was out of their reach, they turned towards Katie. With a howl of rage, the man closest to her raised his war club in a menacing gesture. With his painted face, this man was far more frightening than anything she could have imagined, and Katie knew in an instant that he was going to kill her!

"No…No!" she screamed. The reins slipped unnoticed out of her hand as she backed away in terror.

KATIE, NOT KATJE

Katie was never sure how it happened, but Lawrence was suddenly there. He moved like lightning. In a blur he had the reins, leapt up on the back of the horse, and hauled Katie up behind him. Inches from them the painted enemy was about to pounce. Throwing back its head, the horse pawed the air wildly with his front hooves, and then bolted forward.

A familiar white haze enveloped them. Katie grabbed Lawrence's waist. She could feel the button burning like a hot flame. Flames…tears came to her eyes as she thought of the tiny settlement burned to the ground. She thought of Mevrouw Van Vorst and her family and hoped that they were safe. But there was no way to know.

Now the haze that surrounded them became brighter and brighter. The horse seemed to be racing towards a huge misty ball of white light that appeared up ahead, big enough to swallow them. Pointing at the brilliant light, Lawrence turned to Katie and said, "There lies the doorway to your future, Katje. Your heart sees clearly now. You know you can be strong… You must follow your heart, Katie."

He called me Katie, not Katje, she thought excitedly. And then, the horse sprang into the light.

THE BUTTON

"Katie? Katie, can you hear me?"

Katie heard the gentle voice coming from what seemed like far away. She tried to open her eyes and sit up, but a sharp pain in her head stopped her.

"Mevrouw...I told you... you have to leave now! Take your family across the river to the Glen House..." Katie's voice was weak but urgent. She realized that the awful sounds and smells of the massacre had faded, leaving in their place a strong smell that reminded her of a doctor's office. She lay still and tried to identify the unfamiliar sounds. There was quiet movement all around and a steady, high-pitched beeping coming from something close by. "Katie?" repeated the gentle voice. "You're going to be all right now."

"Anna?" In spite of the pain in her head, Katie forced herself to open her eyes. A worried face swam into focus. "What happened? How did I get here?"

Anna smiled at her reassuringly. "You hit your head when you fell off the horse. The doctors want to keep you here at the hospital a little longer, just for observation. You have a nasty bump on your head. Oh, Katie, it could have been so much worse..."

Katie's heart lurched as she remembered her mother's death after her fall off the horse. And then she searched Anna's face. She saw the concern and love in Anna's eyes. With a jolt she realized that her stepmother reminded her of Mevrouw Van Vorst. Both had the same kind, caring look, the same gentleness. Katie had always been too angry to notice that look on Anna's face before. She reached out for Anna's hand. "I was so afraid I'd never see you and Dad again…"

Anna leaned over and hugged Katie. "Your father and I were so worried about you. We both love you very much, you know." She cleared her throat and straightened up. "Speaking of your father, I'd better go get him. He was talking with your doctor." At the door Anna turned back. She hesitated, "Katie, when you were waking up, you called me 'Mevrouw'… you mumbled something about saving a family. What did you mean?"

Katie thought for a second and then said, "Anna, Mevrouw was someone who reminds me of you. She's someone who was a good mother and she was very kind to me." Katie paused, "She helped my heart to see clearly." Anna looked confused for a moment. She walked back to the bed slowly and gently stroked Katie's hair.

"You know that I love you, Katie," she said softly and then with a smile she left the room.

Katie awoke the next morning in her own comfortable bed. Sunlight was streaming into her room. Gingerly touching the tender bump on her head, she wondered, *Did I dream it or did I really go back in time?* Throwing back the covers, she got up and stood at the window.

"Hey, Lawrence!" she said from habit...and then she remembered. "The button! Where's my button?" Katie realized it was not around her neck where it should be.

Hurrying to the bundled-up costume she had left in a heap on the floor the night before, she reached into the pocket. As her hand closed over the familiar object, she breathed a sigh of relief. It made her think of her strange experience with the portrait on the stairs the night of her birthday dinner. She headed for the portrait, still clutching the button in her hand.

"I'm glad you're up, Katie. How are you feeling?" said Mr. Van Epps as he came up the stairs.

"I'm fine, Dad," Katie said, her eyes still looking at the portrait.

"By the way, the nurse took this off when you had your x-rays yesterday. I've been keeping it for you." Katie turned to see what her father was holding. She gasped when she saw her button dangling from the snippet of yarn. "What happened to the nice chain we gave you?" Mr. Van Epps questioned.

" I-I'm sorry, but it got broken, Dad." Katie stammered. Her heart was pounding and with a trembling hand she took the dangling button from her father. The other button was still clutched in her hand. She realized what having the two buttons meant: she really had gone back in time! Abruptly she turned back to the portrait and asked, "Exactly who is this, Dad? And how did you say she's related to me?"

Pleased that his daughter was finally showing some interest in their family history, Mr. Van Epps said, "Well, she was your eleventh great grandmother on your mother's side." He turned and started down the stairs, then called back over his shoulder, "Oh, and we know her maiden name. It was Helena Van Vorst."

Katie stood alone on the stairway staring with disbelief at the portrait on the wall. Her eyes rested on the lacy gold button that Helena wore on her cloak. This time Katie wasn't surprised when the button in the portrait began to glow. All around her, once again, the stairway was bathed in that eerie, shimmering light. With only the slightest hesitation, she took a deep breath, slipped the circle of yarn over her head, and felt the familiar warmth of the button.

"Now I know who you really are," she whispered, looking into Helena's eyes. Instantly the glowing button in the portrait disappeared.

GLOSSARY

1. **ancestors** Relative on your mother's or father's side of the family from whom you are descended by birth

2. **clapboard** Wooden board used for siding a house

3. **cloak** Coat without sleeves that wraps around the shoulders and hangs to the knees and wrists

4. **colonial** Describing people, places and things during the period of time before the American Revolution

5. **comforter** Quilt or bed covering

6. **Dominie** ("dom un ee") Dutch term for leader of a church

7. **gable** Upper part of a building wall between the sloping sides of the roof

8. **garret** Room just below the roof of a house, formed by the slope of the roof; an attic

9. **garrison** Group of soldiers living in a town in order to defend it

10. **Goeden avond** ("gud en ah vond") Dutch for "good evening"

11. **Goeden dag** ("gud en doc") Dutch for "good day"

12. **Goeden morgan** ("gud en mor gun") Dutch for "good morning"

13. **gourd** Roundish, hard-shelled fruit of a plant in the squash family, sometimes dried with seeds inside

14. **hearth** Hard, flat stone surface beneath a fireplace, that extends out into a room

15. **homespun** Homemade cloth that is woven on a loom

16. **keg** Small wooden barrel

17. **massacre** Attack during which a group of people are slaughtered

18. **Mevrouw** ("meh vrow") Dutch term for "Mrs."

19. **Minjheer** ("mine heer") Dutch term for "Mister"

20. **pocket** Cloth bag, hung at the waist, often used to hold needles, thread, and other important items

21. **porridge** Oatmeal boiled in water or milk

22. **samp** Corn pounded then boiled until crusty; sometimes cooked with salt beef or pork, potatoes, and other roots like carrots and turnips

23. **Schoonectendel** ("skoon ek ten dal") Dutch for beautiful, valuable piece of land. Thought by some to be the origin of the name, "Schenectady"

24. **settle** Long wooden bench or seat with a high back and arms

25. **snippet** Small piece cut from something; for example, a snippet of yarn

26. **stockade** Tall wooden fence built for protection

27. **stoop** Platform with steps, and sometimes seats, at the door of a house.

28. **tallow** Animal fat melted down for making candles

29. **tankard** Large mug usually made from metal or wood, sometimes with an attached cover

30. **tercentennial** The three hundredth anniversary of an event

31. **thatch** A plant material (like straw) used as a sheltering cover especially of a house.

32. **tonic** Homemade medicine made to drink

33. **trundle** Low bed that can be pushed under a larger bed when it is not being used

34. **warming pan** Long handled, flat, round pan filled with hot coals and used for heating a bed

Printed in the United States
67760LVS00002B/148-246